MAGNETIC ATTRACTION

REAGAN HAWK
MANDY M. ROTH

RAVEN HAPPY HOUR, LLC

Magnetic Attraction (Cyborg Desires) © Copyright 2017, Reagan Hawk

First Electronic Printing 2006

ALL RIGHTS RESERVED.

All books are copyrighted to the author and may not be resold or given away without written permission from the author, Mandy M. Roth.

This novel is a work of fiction and intended for mature audiences only. Any and all characters, names, events, places and incidents are used under the umbrella of fiction and are of the author's imagination and should not be confused with fact. Any resemblance to persons, living or dead, or events or places or locales is merely coincidence.

Published by Raven Happy Hour LLC
Oxford, MS USA
Raven Happy Hour LLC and all affiliate sites and projects are © Copyrighted 2004-2017

DEDICATION

To the one I love. We're never handed what we can't handle.

BLURB

Magnetic Attraction (Cyborg Desires Book 2)

No matter how many light years you travel, the past is never far behind. Tired of a life on the run, Kiwi has put down roots on a science vessel. She finds more than she bargained for in the form of cocksure, overachieving, too-sexy-for-his-own-good Dr. Conell Ballou. His arrogance is infuriating--which, strangely, makes her want him more.

Since the tiny spitfire of a mechanic boarded his vessel, Conell hasn't been able to focus on much of anything except her. Kiwi's mere presence pulses through every synthetic and humanoid part of his body. And, unknown to both Kiwi and Conell, her past is entwined with his.

But a deranged captain of the Vanos, the alien race from which they're defending mankind, is still hunting for Kiwi. Against all the odds, Conell and Kiwi have a second chance at happiness--if the enemy doesn't find them first.

ONE

Orbiting Planet Rhesus in the Prometheus Quadrant of the A-QPT46 System...

"PEGASUS'S BALLS," Kiwi cursed softly as she twisted the last torque nut into place. The couplings had needed replacing, and once there, she'd realized her ship's thrusters were in need of work too. The exothermic reaction sections of the engine had seen better days as well. Still, she made do. Her ship was a thing of pride to her. It represented freedom, regardless how pristine it was—or wasn't, in her case. In the scope of the fleet, her cargo ship wasn't the worst. Not by far. Out of necessity she'd learned to do her own repairs. It wasn't a glamorous life, but it was hers to do with as she pleased. Besides, since she'd taken up residency on the science vessel, which had been created to house a thousand, Kiwi found life wasn't nearly as hard as it had been on her own.

Still, laying down roots wasn't her style, regardless how right the situation seemed to be. Not anymore. There had been a time she would have, but that was before the attack—when she was a different person. A person who thought she was entitled to everything and worked for nothing.

That girl is long gone.

Kiwi shimmied out from the smoky gray shaft, her palms sliding over the slick surface. She double-checked the work she'd spent the last three hours doing, before exiting her personal ship. The thruster engines had required a complete overhaul, and she'd needed something to keep herself occupied. Her thoughts had been on a man she shouldn't be worried about. For some reason, she couldn't help herself.

The weight of someone's stare made her backside burn and her face flushed with the knowledge of who was there—the same man

MAGNETIC ATTRACTION 3

she'd been working overtime to not think about. She smiled, still facing the ship. "Enjoying the view?"

"You have no idea."

She hopped to her feet and used a hand to steady herself. The exterior of her cargo ship was smooth to the touch. Almost as smooth as one Dr. Conell Ballou, who happened to be standing directly behind her. She wasn't sure how long he'd been there, but if how hot her ass felt was any indication, he'd either been there a while or was looking damned hard at her. Whenever he was around, she had issues keeping her body temperature regulated. Hot flashes were a constant threat.

His sandy-blond hair flopped down over emerald green eyes, and the faintest hint of a beard showed on his face. He was always in need of a shave. The look suited him. There wasn't much about the man that didn't seem just right. Except for his attitude, of course. He was some sort of super genius and his ego was even bigger than his IQ, and that was saying something.

Last she knew, Conell had been planetside, doing recon work and posing as one of the enemy. With a planet as large as the one they were orbiting, it was entirely possible to drop by and blend in, seemingly unnoticed. It wasn't as if the enemy had taken total control of the planet—yet. They were only in the starting phases of the act. The Vanos weren't to be toyed with, and if left unchecked, they would rid the universe of anyone other than their own kind.

Kiwi hated when Conell volunteered to go on missions that put him on the front line of danger, mainly because his background was that of an academic, not a soldier. Though time and the pending war had hardened him slightly. It hardened everyone it touched. Including her.

"Thought you weren't due back for three more days." She was more than excited to see him but refused to show any sign of it. Whatever was happening between them was coming to a head. She knew it and suspected he did as well.

A devilish grin slid over his entirely too-kissable lips. "Keeping track of me?"

Wiping her grease-covered hands on the back of her overalls, Kiwi stared at him, fighting

MAGNETIC ATTRACTION 5

the driving need to touch him. "Did you want something, Ballou?"

His hungry gaze moved over her and she had a fairly good idea of what he wanted. Problem was, she wanted it too. Getting involved with him wasn't an option. Kiwi had too many secrets she needed to keep under wraps to let anyone too close, and Conell was a man she could see herself opening up to. He wasn't the only one on the ship. That scared her.

Dr. Aeron Braxton-Fairbanks was an amazing woman who had given Kiwi her life back by rebuilding some of the damage the Vanos had inflicted upon her, and even Aeron didn't know all of Kiwi's secrets. She wasn't sure anyone ever would. So many people aboard the vessel weren't what they appeared to be. Many were composed of synthetic parts. Some were part Vanos. Others full Vanos. They'd found a way to get along well enough and had become an odd sort of family. That being said, Kiwi still couldn't imagine telling them everything, even though she knew they wouldn't look at her differently—it was how she viewed herself that left her keeping to herself.

Conell's green gaze slid lower and Kiwi almost asked if he was mentally undressing her. Knowing Conell, he'd only say yes and leave her on the spot—again. He tended to run away whenever a revelation about the need between them came to light.

"You about done for the day?" He cast a sexy grin in her direction and it was all Kiwi could do to keep from biting a knuckle and moaning. The man's voice alone brought her close to orgasm. Add in the rest of the packaging and Conell required her full concentration to ignore.

She glanced at the mounted timekeeper and realized her shift, for lack of a better word, had ended several hours ago. "I guess. But I'd like to finish fitting the thermal—"

"Some of the crew are headed planetside to find a watering hole and relax."

By watering hole, he meant a bar, she was sure of it.

Kiwi almost declined, as she normally did whenever the invitation was presented. She nodded and Conell actually took the smallest of steps backwards.

"Really?"

"Unless you don't want me. The look you're giving me now makes me wonder."

"No. I want you." He cleared his throat. "I mean, *we* want you to come *with* us."

"Do I have time to get cleaned up?"

He beamed. "You sure do."

TWO

Conell brought the passenger shuttle to a port and docked her with ease. Kiwi even looked impressed with his abilities. Prior to her coming into his life, he'd only piloted one size of vessel and hadn't done an exactly stellar job with that. It had been a long-running joke between Kiwi, Aeron and her husband, Brad. They liked to razz Conell about the time he'd sideswiped a fueling station and the time he'd forgotten he was still hooked to said station, ripping a huge chunk of it into orbit. Thanks to Kiwi's tutelage, he could now fly whatever was presented to him. Well, almost anything. Kiwi's cargo ship was strictly off-limits to him or anyone else. She was the only one who piloted it, and any who asked found themselves on the receiving end of a pointed stare. It wasn't as though her ship was in prime condition. It had seen better days, but it was hers, and Conell guessed she liked knowing she could go anytime she wanted. What she didn't know was that he'd follow her to the ends of the universe.

He'd considered offering to let her fly his ship, which was docked in the oversized vessel bay aboard the main ship, but he worried the gesture might be taken the wrong way by her. The last thing he wanted was for Kiwi to feel he was trying to bargain for her affections, but he'd noticed the way she admired his ship from afar. It was indeed a fine vessel, but Conell took it, like so many of the things in his life prior to Kiwi, for granted.

The twelve-man vessel they were currently aboard was filled to the max with crewmembers itching to go planetside to blow off steam. They enjoyed hanging out during downtime aboard the main ship, but every once in a while they simply needed a change of scenery. They also liked being able to pick up females and a little action. Yes, there were women aboard the vessel, but the men outnumbered them five to one. It had also been over a month without any

MAGNETIC ATTRACTION   11

direct enemy contact. The sad truth was, most of the people who joined the crew had a rather ugly history with the Vanos—they had either suffered a loss, had been their prisoner or had defected from their ranks. Any way you turned it, the Vanos were enemies and most of the crewmembers wanted proof what they were doing was working. That proof tended to come in the form of fighting with the Vanos. Conell didn't necessarily agree with the philosophy, but the more he learned about Kiwi's rather guarded past, the more he wanted to kill as many of the enemy as possible.

Conell looked longingly at Kiwi, wondering what had prompted her to say yes to his invite. He was damn happy she had, but all the times he'd asked before, she'd given him lame excuses. She would rush off to be with Aeron or simply vanish before Conell could corner her once more. She'd not only given in to him, she'd met him directly outside his quarters prior to leaving. He'd walked out, taken one look at her, and known he wouldn't be able to stop himself this evening. If the opportunity to be with her, to touch her intimately presented itself, he would seize the moment.

The others exited the vessel swiftly and Conell waited, walking with Kiwi. She had on a pair of skintight tan pants, matching boots and a light green fitted shirt that looked as if it were a second skin on her. Her breasts were on the smaller side, but that was how he preferred them. Most everything about Kiwi was on the smaller side. He found himself concerned that if he did get her to bend to his will, he'd break her with one thrust. Still, picturing her tiny body wrapped around his cock was one of his favorite fantasies. Another was watching her ride him, her hair draping down and over their bodies as he cupped her breasts.

Tonight her long hair was down, grazing the top of her ass. It varied in shade from medium brown to white blonde on the top and sides. Aeron, a woman he considered one of his closest friends, had told him once how very much Kiwi disliked her hair. Conell couldn't fathom why. He often closed his eyes, imagining himself sliding his fingers through it before taking hold and fucking her senseless.

The boarding guards at the station watched Kiwi as she walked past. The hungry looks they cast in her direction had Conell growling, knowing how intimidating he appeared. He was half-Vanos, meaning he was over six and a half feet tall and all muscle. It was in his genetic makeup. It also helped that thirty percent of his body was droid, rebuilt after a vicious attack. He was now even stronger than the Vanos blood had made him—a man most didn't want to cross.

The guards exchanged nervous looks before averting their gazes from Kiwi. Pride welled in Conell as he followed close behind the tiny stick of dynamite. While she wasn't technically his woman, everyone aboard their ship knew his feelings for her. Well, everyone but Kiwi. The men knew better than to make a move on her for fear they'd have to deal with him. The women aboard the main ship had stopped trying to entice him when word of his feelings for Kiwi spread among them.

Too bad Kiwi paid no mind to gossip or spent much time on the crew decks. She tinkered with her ship and hung out with Aeron. Beyond that, she confined herself to her quarters. Conell was determined to chase the loneliness from her brown eyes.

The darkened passageway on the *Rhesus*

watering hole reminded him of a number of dives he'd frequented in his life. Though, in the past he hadn't there to enjoy himself, but rather to retrieve his brother, who'd had a thing for liquor and women. At least Darrin had prior to three years ago. It was at that time Conell stopped having to hunt his brother down on planets notorious for outlaws. It wasn't his job to keep track of his brother. Besides, if you looked at his brother's job, one would assume he was the model of responsibility. That always struck Conell as amusing since Darrin was a decorated Star Union officer. Apparently, the Star Union didn't see drinking and womanizing as a pitfall in their leaders.

Always comforting to know the men sworn to protect you have morals.

"You coming, Ballou?" Kiwi asked, her sultry voice chasing thoughts of anything but her from his head.

He locked gazes with her and grinned. "If I'm lucky, I'll be coming before the night is out."

With a roll of her eyes and flick of her wrist, Kiwi dismissed him. Even with the rejection still fresh on the air, Conell fell into step alongside her, his hand finding her mid-back, escorting her as if she truly was his woman.

Several maintenance droids approached, offering to shine Conell's boots and whisk Kiwi away for a massage. These droids were first-level ones, betas from over a hundred years ago when anything with synthetic parts still resembled a pile of metals rather than a humanoid. The history logs were full of misconceptions about the future—people convinced medicine and technology would never be able to be so intertwined as they now were. Clearly, those people had been wrong. As wrong as those who once believed their planet was alone in the universe or that their planet was flat, rather than round.

Dated droids were common on the outer limits of the quadrants. So were criminals, prostitutes, hustlers, the poor and Vanos. It was a catchall for the unwanted and unsavory.

The droids finally stopped their badgering when Conell and Kiwi approached the main courtyard of the facility. Conell looked up, the glass ceiling provided a stunning view. It was currently of a moonlit night. The holographic image faltered, showing the true sky above them, a blanket of dark purple clouds, before popping back up with the view of night. Either was stunning and pleasing to the eye, but since the sky never changed appearance, Conell imagined the locals enjoyed the change of scenery.

Two Vanos guards walked in their direction and Conell drew Kiwi to him, dipping down and nuzzling his face to her ear, making it look as if they were lovers. The guards would assume Conell was the same as them—a full-blooded warrior for their side. Kiwi was all he worried about. An unclaimed female in the outer quadrants was considered free pickings for the Vanos. Kiwi stepped closer to him, making his cock harden as her scent wafted upwards. Something about her natural smell drove him wild. It was light, slightly floral, but with something he couldn't put his finger on—something that made him want to sink to the floor and cram his cock into her until release.

The touch of her tiny hand on his chest made pre-come seep from his dick. He unashamedly adjusted himself and heard Kiwi's quick intake of breath. Her fingers caressed him tenderly, kneading at his shirt. He wasn't sure if it was fear of the Vanos that had her doing it or

MAGNETIC ATTRACTION   17

if she actually wanted him. At that moment, he didn't care.

Her lips grazed his jawline as he continued to bend to meet her level. She slid her hands to his upper arms and he could have sworn she kissed his cheek before whispering, "Are they gone yet?"

He'd all but forgotten about the Vanos guards.

Lifting his head just enough to peek, he found they were long gone. "Yes."

She didn't pull away at first and neither did he. The fact left Conell grinning like a fool. It was a small sign that Kiwi might be attracted to him as well.

"Ballou," a fellow crewmember shouted. "We saved you two seats."

He cursed under his breath as Kiwi yanked away from him as if he were carrying something contagious.

THREE

Kiwi's pulse raced as she turned, heading in the direction of the bar the crew had selected. Since bars lined the courtyard, she was surprised they'd all selected the same one and was frankly disappointed. As selfish as it sounded, she wanted alone time with Conell, even if she had no intention of acting on the way he made her feel.

She hesitated and Conell took her by the elbow. "Kiwi, you all right?"

"I'm fine," she lied. "Lead the way."

He glanced in the direction of the waiting shipmate and then waved his hand. "Go ahead. We'll catch up with you in a bit."

"Suit yourselves," the man said. "It's packed though."

Kiwi glanced up at Conell, wondering how he'd known she didn't want to share him.

A grin lacking any sign of manipulation met her. He motioned with his head around the courtyard. "Which one looks good to you? Unless...uh...you want to hang out with everyone else."

She smiled and did her best to wipe it from her face as she nudged him. "You pick."

"All right then." He pointed to a bar with a blue sign in a language she couldn't read. "How about that one?"

"Perfect."

He led her to it and spoke with the bouncer at the door. Unlike Conell, Kiwi didn't have a translator chip embedded in her. But she suspected that even without the chip he could hold conversations with a good many other races. He was what he claimed to be, exceedingly smart. He was handsome as hell in his current getup. The stretchy material of his black shirt molded to his every muscle, making her mouth water and drawing attention to his slim waist.

The moment he pushed his floppy blond hair back from his face, Kiwi sighed. The

MAGNETIC ATTRACTION   21

bouncer motioned them through and Conell took her hand in his. He strolled past the clientele as if he owned the place, blending perfectly. Kiwi had to practically run to keep up, because what was an unhurried pace to him, with his long, powerful legs, was a slight jog to her.

Conell glanced back at her and slowed his pace. "Sorry."

"It's okay." She refused to let go of his hand.

The bar was darker than many others she'd been in, and the second she spotted a long stage, she understood what type of bar it was—a strip club.

"Ballou, you brought me to a..." The question died on her lips as a nearly naked man walked onstage, twirling sticks of fire as he did some sort of ritualistic dance, thumping his body along the way.

Conell waved his hand before her face. "Eyes on me, Kiwi."

A giggle erupted from her. "Okay, but can you twirl fire while wearing nothing but a loincloth? That's damn hard to beat."

Before he could answer, a sexy, part-humanoid female approached, carrying a tray of drinks. She spoke and her voice carried with it a buzz, charging the air. Kiwi had heard of species that could induce sexual desire with nothing more than their voice. She kept a keen eye as the men immediately surrounding them stopped what they were doing and stared at the woman with longing looks. Conell, on the other hand, merely glanced at her, grabbed two of the house drinks from the tray and nodded his thanks.

The pale blue lighting splashed over his squared face. Kiwi reached past the drink he held out to her and straight to his jaw. She touched it lightly, her fingers brushing his lips before she jerked to her senses, pulling her hand away.

Conell bent, putting a drink in her hand. The edges of his full lips twitched and Kiwi knew he was fighting a smile. Taking the drink from him, she averted her gaze, hoping he'd avoid mentioning how she'd caressed him for no reason.

She took a large gulp of the drink and stiffened as it burned its way down her throat. She coughed and Conell laughed. "Did you poison me?"

"Hardly," he said, his face suddenly closer to

hers. "But I should warn you. The drinks they serve here are laced with something that acts as a type of aphrodisiac to the Vanos and several other races. Don't worry, straight humans aren't included, but you should keep an eye on me. If I start getting a little too…" he grinned, "…fresh, feel free to use that arm of yours to knock me on my ass."

Kiwi froze. One of the many secrets she'd spent so long keeping nagged at her. She wasn't a full human. She was like Conell, half-Vanos, though it was difficult to believe because she lacked almost all the traits used to visually identify one.

"Conell."

"Yes?" He took a sip of her drink.

She watched as he swallowed, the muscles in his neck moving. Kiwi decided to let fate do what it wanted, at least for tonight. Tomorrow was another day.

Conell headed to the back of the bar and she stayed close on his heels. When he settled into a darkened corner booth, she followed, easing in alongside him. Her gaze went to the fire dancer and she realized he no longer had on a loincloth. He now twirled his sticks of fire while completely naked. His cock was flaccid, yet large and his body looked to be carved from stone.

Her eyes widened. "If he's not careful, he'll lose something vital."

Conell's deep laugh reverberated through her and she found herself leaning, resting her body against his as she sipped her drink. He didn't protest but rather drank, watching the show. When a set of female dancers joined the naked male, Kiwi tensed, a spike of jealously flaring through her. She didn't want Conell looking at naked women. She wanted him looking at her.

At me? I've lost my mind.

Conell's hand brushed over hers and Kiwi gulped, their gazes colliding. She didn't jerk her hand away. She left it in place, enjoying the feel of his thumb easing back and forth on it.

Another sexy waitress approached with a tray of drinks, taking Conell's almost empty one and replacing it with a full. Kiwi stared in awe as he downed the second drink quickly.

"Uh, Ballou, you do realize if you go nuts and try to hump one of the women here, I'm

MAGNETIC ATTRACTION   25

not strong enough to get you under control—droid arm or not. You're huge."

With a wagggle of his brows, he put his face close to hers. "So, what you're saying is, I'm too much for you to handle?"

She knew what he meant, and instead of blushing like she normally would, she met his gaze head-on. "I'm tougher than I look, Ballou."

The bizarre music pumping throughout the club reached new heights and Kiwi stared at the stage, unable to believe what she was seeing. The female dancers were on their knees, taking turns licking the male dancer's long cock as he continued to twirl sticks of fire high in the air. She couldn't tear her gaze away as they stroked the man, fondling his sac, then his shaft, seeming to live for the act.

Conell touched her chin, forcing her gaze to him. "If I'd known you'd be so interested in him, I wouldn't have brought you here. I'd have picked a different bar." His jaw clenched. "Kiwi, you may need to call some of the crew over here soon."

"Why?"

"Because if I see you looking at that guy on

stage again, while I sense how fucking turned on you are, I am going to kill him."

She grabbed his hand. "Hey, I was just watching the show."

"How about…" He put his face close to hers and she could smell the drink upon his breath. "You keep those brown eyes on me instead." His mouth covered hers and everything else faded away. Their tongues laced and Kiwi found herself inching towards him, practically crawling on his lap. This was so wrong but felt so right. She shouldn't get attached or allow whatever was between them to escalate to this level. She needed to have no strings in her life. It made running much easier and kept everyone around her safe. Already she'd formed a friendship with Aeron. Sex with Conell would take complicated to a completely new level.

The thoughts in her head were rational. The movements of her body, of her mouth, were anything but. She found herself gripping the back of his neck, returning his kiss with so much passion it shocked her.

He lifted her, settling her on his lap as his hands found their way to her backside. Heat ignited deep within her and a light sheen of sweat broke out over her skin. She attributed it, and her overwhelming desire, to the drink. She swept her tongue over his, moaning.

Conell tugged at the back of her hair, forcing her body to arch into him. Her diamond-like nipples scraped over his chest, and the very action caused her pussy to cream. She rocked on his lap, the distended flesh between his legs pushing against her clit, making a beg hover on her lips.

Moans from the dancers onstage mixed with her own and Kiwi sucked on Conell's tongue. He yanked her shirt free of her pants and slid his hands under it. As his fingers found her nipples, she tensed, remembering they weren't alone.

"B-Ballou," she panted. "Anyone could see us."

Nodding, he continued to kiss at her neck while tweaking her nipples, making her protests fade away. She put her hands on his shoulders to keep her balance as she tipped her head back, enjoying his touch. Cool air hit her breasts and it took Kiwi a second to realize he'd hiked her shirt up. His warm lips enveloped her nipple and pleasure centered in the pit of her stomach, desperate to break free. She writhed on him, grinding her mound to his clothed cock.

He paid equal attention to her other nipple and she dug her fingers into his shoulder. He pulled off and stared at her, his gaze hungry. "Turn around."

"What?" she asked, confused.

"I said—" he lifted her and faced her the other way as if she were nothing more than a rag doll, "—turn around."

She obeyed, turning, sitting on him with her back facing his front. This dominant side of Conell excited her even though she believed herself past the days of allowing a man to command her. He pushed on her upper back, forcing her to bend over the table as he remained seated. Kiwi pulled her shirt down, covering her breasts, noticing all eyes around them were focused on the stage as the male dancer thrust his cock into one of the females while the other parted his ass cheeks and licked at his cleft.

Conell eased his fingers into the top of her pants and dragged them down. He tugged on her shirt so it covered her from the view of others and she looked back to see him fondling

MAGNETIC ATTRACTION   29

the front of his pants, unzipping them with his other hand. He locked gazes with her as he slipped a long finger between her legs, dipping into her heated core.

His entire body seemed to stiffen. "Stellar stars, you're tight and wet."

Reason began to work its way into her brain. She shook her head and tried to move away from him. Conell kept her in place with ease.

"No. We're done when I say we are."

"Conell?" she asked, a streak of fear darting through her.

He caressed her inner thigh, seeming to collect himself as he took a deep breath. "I would never hurt you, Kiwi." He swallowed hard. "I'm still in control enough to stop this. Tell me now or…"

Reaching down, she took hold of his wrist and pushed his hand to her pussy. He took the hint and inserted his finger again, working it in and out of her, making the pleasure build. When he withdrew his finger, she whimpered.

FOUR

Chuckling, Conell pulled on her hips, easing her down and over the head of his massive cock. The girth alone stretched Kiwi to the point she yelped. Conell kept hold of her, keeping her from driving down on him too hard as he reached around, stroking her clit. He bit his lower lip to keep from coming when he was only barely inside her. He rubbed her swollen bud and eased in more. She forced herself down onto him farther, taking him inch by painfully slow inch. By the time he was in to the hilt, Conell was sweating and gritting his teeth to stave off his orgasm.

She leaned back, turning her head and meeting his mouth with hers, almost making him explode inside her. Their tongues danced, circling around one another as Kiwi moved, up and down, controlling the pace and depth she took him. It was a sweet torture that Conell was willing to endure for the time being. He continued to rub her clit. She stiffened on him, the walls of her channel clamping down on his cock.

He took hold of her hips, driving her down onto him as he thrust upward. Kiwi cried out, causing patrons to glance in their direction. She didn't seem to notice and Conell didn't give a shit who watched them. He was where he wanted to be—in her. Besides, she was covered from their prying eyes. It was obvious what they were doing, but if anyone wanted to witness penetration or exposed flesh, they'd have to watch the stage show. He wasn't fine with the idea of them seeing his woman's naked body.

My woman.

The thought spurred him on as he continued to pound into her grasping, wet flesh. Kiwi smacked her hands down onto the table, moaning loudly. The hand that had been partially rebuilt left a hairline crack running through the table.

Conell returned to kissing her mouth,

amused that she was indeed stronger than she appeared to be. He struck a steady rhythm, assuming he'd be able to last longer now that he was primed, but when Kiwi reached down and took hold of his balls, he lost his train of thought. Ramming into her, he jerked as she cried out again. He jetted seed deep within her, his cock twitching as his jaw went slack.

She made a move to slide off him but he held her in place. "No." He pressed his mouth to her ear. "Stay."

Much to his delight, she didn't argue. She settled into place and leaned her head back, resting against him. The act told him that he'd not only gained her body, he'd gained her trust as well.

It didn't take long for Conell to be ready for another round. He began to pump into her, slowly at first before driving in hard. She clung to the table with one hand and his thigh with the other, taking everything he dished out to her. He made it all the way through another stage act, this one consisting of two men taking pleasure from one another. Kiwi came several times. Each time she cried out, unabashed, before finally looking back at him. The very sight of her brown eyes on him and the look of satisfaction left him finishing in her.

She eased off him and he helped her pull her pants up before bothering with his own. Conell waited, worried she'd sit far from him or, worse yet, storm off, upset things had gone as far as they had between them. When she turned and sat on his lap, wrapping her arms around his neck and putting her cheek to his shoulder, he exhaled, fearful of breaking the moment.

She tipped her head up and kissed his lips softly. "I need to hit the head and clean up."

With as long and hard as he'd come in her, that wasn't shocking news. Nodding, he lifted her and set her on her feet before making a move to stand as well.

Kiwi grinned. "I can make it to the little girls' room and back all on my own, Ballou."

"I know, but this isn't the kind of establishment one lets their woman walk around in unescorted."

She lifted a brow. "Am I your woman?"

"Damn straight," he said, grinning like a fool.

Kiwi laughed and shook her head. "I'll be

MAGNETIC ATTRACTION   35

right back. Try to hold off on drinking anything else. I'm going to need time to recover."

She'd only just left when he heard a commotion coming from outside the club in the courtyard. He stood quickly and made his way to the entrance just in time to see a group of Vanos males harassing several of his fellow crewmembers.

Without thought for how he was going to take on five Vanos at one time, Conell rushed into the fray.

FIVE

Captain Ajos watched the woman with the long, flowing hair and the wide brown eyes as the man she was with drew her onto his lap. From the expression on her face, she was being fucked. Ajos fisted his drink, fighting the need to rush to her and rip her from her lover's lap. She was his woman. He knew it. It didn't matter that her hair was darker than it had been a year and a half ago or that her body no longer bore the proof of her resistance, she was the one he'd selected to stand by his side. He'd worked hard, breaking her spirit and claiming her for his own. She'd been foolish, thinking she could stand against the likes of him—a Vanos captain and decorated war hero.

She'd come to him, so full of vigor, believing

the universe was created to serve her. He'd beat that out of her, making her understand she was no better than him. In fact, the proof of her blood tests showed she was a lesser—a half-blood. Part human and part Vanos.

He smiled, remembering the look upon her face as he told her the news that her biological parents were not the ones who raised her. Her father, whom she'd held in such high regard, had spent her life lying to her. As powerful as he was, he wasn't stronger than Ajos.

She panted, gripping the table before her as nothing short of wonder covered her face. She liked the cock in her and wanted more. That alone made Ajos want to punish her for her betrayal of him. The fact she'd managed to escape from him a year and half ago still weighed heavily on him. She shouldn't have been able to outsmart his guards. She shouldn't have been able to make her way off the base she'd been held at, and she shouldn't have left him.

But she had.

Fate apparently wanted her with him, or else she wouldn't have shown up at the dive where he'd decided to allow his men to take much-

MAGNETIC ATTRACTION   39

needed relaxation time. Here she was, within reach, riding a man who he knew had to be Vanos.

How dare she betray me with one of my own.

The stage show changed, moving from two females pleasuring a male flame twirler to two men. Ajos watched as one of the men slid down the length of the other, raking his fingers over the man's torso. When he reached the man's thick cock, he bent, licking a long line over it.

Ajos's dick hardened as well. He reached down and undid his pants, freeing himself. He stroked, his gaze settling on the men onstage. The man on his knees took the other deep to the back of his throat, gagging slightly before pulling off, a look of joy in his eyes. He twisted, going to his hands and knees for the crowd to see the side of him. The tall blond walked around behind him, caressing his wet cock as he bent. The man lined up perfectly with the redhead on his hands and knees. With one thrust, the man was buried in the other's ass, tipping his head back and crying out.

Ajos jerked on his cock, his attention moving back to the woman who was his. From the look upon her face, she was coming. He stilled before yanking hard, loving the pain as he raked his nails over the smooth flesh of his shaft, coming under the table, seeing himself buried deep in her pussy.

"Captain," one of his men said, standing near him.

Ajos had not heard the man's approach and cared little that he was caught in the act of pleasing himself. He watched as she stood, then sat upon the man's lap, whispering something to him before motioning towards the back of the bar.

Perfect.

Soon, when the time was right, he would have alone time with her. Making a rash move without knowing the full extent of her backing, if indeed she had any, was foolish.

He gave the guard a hard stare then grinned. "You have perfect timing. See that man there?" He pointed to the fool stupid enough to fuck what was his. "Watch him closely. Lure him away from the female."

The guard's eyes widened. "Sir, that is the woman who—"

"I know who she is. Do as I say!"

Nodding, the guard disappeared into the

crowd, leaving Ajos to await the opportunity to see her again. He followed behind her, watching as she made her way towards the restrooms. He stuck to the shadows, hungry for her, but acting too soon could jeopardize so much more than just losing her.

I want the bastard foolish enough to touch her as well. I want him at my mercy, begging me to end his suffering. He will understand who is the superior when I am through with him, and he will know she is mine.

She entered the restrooms and he moved closer, opening the door and following behind her. His blood raced through his veins. The knowledge he was close enough to reach out and touch her consumed him. As the sound of the decontamination unit kicked on, he inched even closer, allowing the low buzz to cover the sound of his movements as he stepped onto a side grill and peeked into the stall to watch her.

Ajos reached down the length of himself, palming his erection, thriving on the understanding she was unaware of his presence. There were times before, when she was his, that he would view her through the surveillance feeds during which he either masturbated or fucked another woman, all the while watching her.

He tugged on his covered cock, wanting it to be her hand on him.

Soon.

He could easily take her now, force her to submit and have her sucking his cock off in seconds. She excelled at the task and he often found himself likening other women to her, forcing their mouths down and his cock to the back of their throats, waiting for their gag reflexes to kick in and loving the feeling of their bodies' involuntary reaction to the size of him.

She'd always had a way about her. A certain stare that told him exactly how much she loathed him, yet she served him. It was as close to euphoria as he'd ever encountered and he wanted it back.

Grab her. Take her now.

He stiffened, fighting his own impulses. Giving in now would mean he'd forfeit his chance at collecting the man she'd been with. She was certainly something he desired to have back in his grasp, but the praise and the purse from a successful capture of the man was too tempting. Ajos would end up a very wealthy

MAGNETIC ATTRACTION   43

man indeed. All he had to do was hold off on taking her until the other target could be obtained as well.

Ajos's will was tested as she emerged from a stall, glancing in his direction, her gaze meeting his for a nanosecond. Those beautifully haunted eyes used to reflect hate. Now they showed a hint of fear.

Even better.

She looked away and he retreated quickly with the knowledge he wouldn't have to wait much longer to reclaim what was rightfully his.

To the victor goes the spoils.

SIX

Kiwi entered the bathroom, her body still strumming with sensuality. Her cunt ached sweetly, missing the feel of Conell within her. She glanced into the mirror, shocked she'd given up so easily to the pull and offer of him. She wanted to blame it on the drink and its ability to influence the Vanos side of her, but it wasn't completely at fault. She wanted Conell and had from the moment she'd met him. The combined juices coating her pussy were affirmation enough of just how much she craved him.

She entered a waste-management stall and cleaned herself before walking back out and using the hand-decontamination unit.

Turning, she froze, positive for the briefest of moments that she'd seen the face of a man who had spent a year and half of her life terrorizing her. Her body stiff, her movements jerky, she took a deep, unhurried breath, trying to calm herself. Nothing was there. It was her, alone in the restroom. Shaken, she rubbed her neck, glancing around once more just to be sure.

Nothing.

Kiwi stepped out and made her way back to the table. There was no sign of Conell. The newest act on stage consisted of a man and a *gatarian* farm animal. Her stomach twisted. No part of her wanted to stick around to witness what would transpire on the stage.

"Ballou?"

Apparently, Conell didn't want to watch the sick show either.

Kiwi headed towards the entrance and stopped as she heard the sounds of arguing. She knew the language well since she'd been forced to learn it or forever remain ignorant to what was being said around her while she was held captive in a Vanos prison camp.

The second she heard Conell speaking in

Vanos, she rushed out. He was surrounded by at least eight of them, all huge and all wearing the insignia branding them as military, though they weren't in their uniforms.

"This human is mine," Conell said in Vanos as he pointed towards a fellow crewmember. "Good slave labor is hard to come by."

Kiwi didn't dare correct Conell. She knew he was lying to keep the others safe. She also knew she'd be a liability if she dared enter the equation now. She kept to the back, making her way around, hoping to find the rest of the crewmembers they'd brought down to the planet. She spotted two, doing much the same thing she was. They were full Vanos but had been defectors among their own kind, ashamed of the brutality their people inflicted on anyone different than them. If they stepped forth, they'd risk one of the Vanos enemy knowing one of them and that they were no longer playing for the same side.

She nodded to the men and tried to walk past them. They caught her around the waist and jerked her back, just as two more Vanos guards walked out from a bar. They hid her from view and she patted each on the chest as a means of a silent thank you. Once the coast was clear, Kiwi ducked under her friends and slipped behind a pillar, needing to be closer to Conell in the event assistance was required.

He continued to talk, seemingly having everything under control. When she glanced across the courtyard and thought she caught another glimpse of the man who had made her life a living hell—Captain Ajos—Kiwi gasped, accidentally drawing attention to herself.

Focus. He's not there. It's your mind playing tricks on you.

The guards faced her, as did Conell. Concern flashed through his green eyes. She grinned and waved at him, doing what she'd seen so many Vanos females do to their mates. She walked straight for him and spoke fluently in their native language. "*Delicatico*, you left without telling me. That is a very good way to find your bed cold on this fine evening."

The Vanos guards exchanged looks before stepping back and letting her through. Kiwi glanced back towards her friends and nodded. They knew what to do—be ready for an escape.

Conell yanked her to him, making her

MAGNETIC ATTRACTION   49

breath catch. He splayed his large hand over her abdomen and chuckled, still speaking in Vanos. "If you dared to try to keep me from your bed, I'd be left with no choice but to punish you. Sadly, you'd enjoy that too much. You make a man proud, so long as he's smart enough to hide the weapons before he closes his eyes at night."

The Vanos guards grinned and laughed.

One looked familiar to her and Kiwi's mind raced with where she might have seen him before. When it hit her, she froze. Her spine tingled as remembered pain and fear flooded over her.

Conell must have sensed the change in her because he tugged her even closer and put his lips to her ear. "I won't let any of them hurt you."

She knew he believed his words. The problem was, if she was correct and the guard was who she thought him to be, no one could protect her from his boss.

Captain Ajos.

Bile rose and Kiwi found herself grasping desperately to Conell's hand. She'd wanted to believe it was all her imagination. That Ajos couldn't be there. It appeared she was wrong. Dead wrong if Ajos had anything to do with it.

Just touching Conell made some of the fear and pain of the past disappear. She swayed and Conell kept hold of her. The guards opened the circle slightly and then stopped, looking past Conell at someone Kiwi couldn't see.

The minute the Vanos began to close ranks, the crewmembers Conell had brought with them launched into action, attacking from all sides. The guards found themselves outnumbered, but it didn't stop them from putting up a good fight.

Kiwi gasped as Conell thrust her to his side, protecting her with his massive body as he punched a guard in the face. He turned quickly, striking another. She thrust one away from Conell's blind side a second before he would have leveled Conell. Her rebuilt arm twitched uncontrollably and she grabbed it to her, shrieking in pain. Whatever she'd done, the arm didn't care for.

Conell slowed at the sound of Kiwi's cry of pain. The distraction cost him greatly, leaving him staring down the barrel of a pulse weapon.

His concern was for Kiwi, not himself as he knocked the weapon to the side. It went off, striking the dome covering the courtyard. The hologram fizzed out, sparks flying in every direction. The sound of it cracking warned Conell the structure would indeed go. When it did, it would suck the oxygen out with it. The planet's normal atmosphere was toxic to any and all species reliant upon oxygen.

Snatching a hold of Kiwi, he shouted to his men, alerting them of the danger. The Vanos guards heard as well and although they generally weren't ones to back down from a fight, they too knew the repercussions of remaining in the courtyard. Alarms sounded as bay doors to the varying bars began to close, assuring oxygen remained within each establishment. It was standard operating procedure for any planets maintaining artificial atmospheres. Conell knew they could easily make it to a bar, but he also knew the Vanos would be in the watering station, awaiting the repair to the dome, ready and willing to kill them the minute they could.

"We need to get to the landing hanger!" he shouted.

Kiwi held her rebuilt arm to her tiny body

and nodded, following close behind him. The other crewmembers moved in around them, forming a protective barrier as they made a mad dash to the hanger. The beta droids converged on them again, once more trying to solicit services. Two of the men with the group gave up trying to move the droids out of the way and lifted them, running with them.

They made it through the landing-hanger bay doors a nanosecond prior to them closing. While that was a good thing, it wasn't great. The landing hanger was the first place the facility would pump viable air from to support life within each bar.

Conell motioned to the shuttle vessel and the crewmembers filed in, taking the beta droids with them. Conell spun, lifted Kiwi and ran with her, boarding the vessel as fast as he could. The door shut behind him and he looked to find a trusted member of the team piloting the vessel. Nodding his appreciation, Conell carried Kiwi to the back and sat with her, holding her close, knowing she was in pain and that he was powerless to help her until they were back aboard the main ship.

The ship rocked to the left and Conell knew

MAGNETIC ATTRACTION   53

the dome had given way, causing a force of pressure to rush through the facility. He held Kiwi to him, keeping her steady and safe. The effects of the drinks he'd downed had long since worn off and he was thankful for the added layer of control. Pressing his lips to her forehead, Conell put his hand lightly over her injured arm. The fingers on the hand twitched and he closed his eyes, praying she would be all right. It was documented that not all humans or humanaids bionics remained active at all times. Some did, some did not. It depended upon the bionic itself and the person. Some bodies rejected the additions as far out as a year after introduction. The problem was, Kiwi wouldn't just lose use of her arm; she would lose her life because the rest of her organs had been strengthened with the introduction of the synthetic parts as well, becoming reliant on them.

A soft caress to his cheek left him opening his eyes to find Kiwi watching him. She offered a soft smile. "You really need to stay armed at all times, Ballou. They could have killed you. Do you think talking your way out of everything is the answer? It's not. You could have been—"

He pressed his lips to hers, quieting her.

When he was done, he grinned. "Yes, dear, I'll start carrying a weapon at all times. Thank you for worrying about me."

She huffed and he laughed.

Kiwi shook her head and surrendered against him.

SEVEN

Ajos roared, pounding on the locked bay doors of the hole-in-the-ground bar he'd been forced to dive into when the dome shattered. He'd been so close to having not only her, but others as well. Arriving back at the base with a ship full of possible slave labor, a wanted man and the woman he'd staked claim on would seal his position as a leader among his people.

Now he had no choice but to wait out the repairs to the dome. No living thing could survive the planet's atmosphere. It made for a preferred watering hole and weight station for vagabonds on the outer quadrants. No one other than criminals and those seeking the darker side of life would bother stopping at such an inhospitable planet. Well, aside from him and his men.

One of his men neared him. "Sir, we should have taken the shot on them straightaway. Our hesitation and diversion assisted them in escaping."

Ajos turned to face the man. A sick smile spread slowly over his face and the man took a step back. Ajos filled the gap between them. "You dare to question my orders?"

"N-no, sir. I just… I only wanted to… No, sir."

"You only wanted to what, soldier?" He slipped a hand down and fingered his weapon.

The guard's gaze followed the movement and he swallowed hard, the veins in his neck popping. "I only wanted to tell you that you… you made the right call, sir. Your leadership skills have never been in question."

A crowd had gathered around them but Ajos cared little. He nodded to the guard and watched as the man began to relax.

Ajos drew his weapon fast and pressed it to the guard's head. He pulled the trigger without hesitation and then watched the body fall to the floor. He stared down at it. "And they never will be in question, soldier."

He looked towards his other men, the ones who had scattered into this establishment rather than the neighboring ones. They each wore blank expressions. As they should.

He grinned. "Anyone else care to question me?"

A round of "noes" followed.

"Very well, then clear an area for us to work. We have much planning to do. They may have slipped through our fingers this time, but they won't again. No. Next time we will meet them when they are least expecting it. First things first. I need three men to volunteer to observe them, gather details and the like once we've located them again."

Reluctantly, three of his men stepped forth.

"Good." He lifted a hand. "One more thing. Should any harm come to the female, I will personally handle your punishment."

The men paled.

EIGHT

Kiwi put her set of wrenches down and backed away from her ship. Finally, its repairs were done. Unable to sleep after the debriefing, she'd returned to her ship and worked well through the night, doing what needed done to keep her mind off what had taken place almost a week prior. She'd been good about avoiding Conell, wanting to give him the distance he seemed to need. The only problem with that was how much she missed seeing him. Honestly, she missed touching him as well. Each night since they'd been together she'd lain awake, rubbing her clit, thinking of how he felt buried in her and wishing he didn't regret what had passed between them.

The sound of the bay doors opening and then closing alerted her that she was no longer alone. The hot sensation on her ass told her exactly who was with her.

"Ballou," she said with a puff of air. Excitement mixed with a hefty dose of trepidation moved over her. He hadn't so much as glanced in her direction for over a week, and now he was showing up in her hanger.

"You didn't make it in to see Aeron this morning to check more on that arm," he said, his voice even.

She faced him with a level gaze. "I was busy. Sorry."

"Kiwi, I don't want things between us to be awkward. What happened was right...it was natural."

She lifted a brow in objection. "Fucking in a bar full of people and then not saying so much as two words to one another once we got back is natural? Maybe for you. Not for me, Ballou."

He stepped closer. "That's not what I meant, Kiwi. Don't twist my words."

She huffed. "How can I twist them when you hardly say anything?" Putting her hand up, she motioned for him to go. "Just leave. I'll keep clear of you and I'll be sure to check in with Aeron about my arm later. There, wipe your conscience clear now?"

Conell jerked and stared at the floor. "I don't know what to say."

"How about you say nothing and just leave?"

"How about you shut up and let me think a minute, woman? You've got my thoughts all jumbled into a tangled mess. I'm worried about you to the point I'm bordering on stalking you, all the while I'm afraid you're going to find me and tell me how much of a mistake what happened between us was." He covered his eyes with a hand. "Kiwi, I swore to myself that I'd never let anything happen to you, and the first time trouble comes up, I fail. I'm not proud of that fact and I'm sure not proud of how I took you."

She stared at him, watching as he swept his hands out in a dramatic fashion as he spoke.

"I wanted more for us…for you, actually. I wanted everything to be perfect. To be right. Not to be in some seedy sex bar with people catching glimpses of us."

He continued on and Kiwi simply stood

quietly, letting him. Conell was a passionate man and it was interesting to see a romantic side of him poking through. Aeron, on more than one occasion, had hinted that Conell had been that way prior to the Vanos invasion, but this was the first glimpse Kiwi had of it.

Conell dragged his hands through his shaggy hair, looking tired. "Kiwi, what I'm trying to say is, I'm sorry."

The edges of her mouth drew upwards and she blinked at him. "Ballou, shut up."

He froze.

She moved closer to him. "And kiss me."

Fire lit in his green gaze as he bent, lifting her into the air, putting them eye to eye. "You're not upset with me?"

She touched his jaw. "For a super genius, you sure don't know what 'shut up and kiss me' means."

His mouth clamped down on hers and everything else faded away. Their tongues met and Kiwi moaned, pulling harder on him, needing to be closer to him. Conell had her spun around, her back to the outer part of her ship in no time flat. She ate at his mouth, tugging at his shirt, her entire body tight with need.

Conell bit at her lower lip, driving Kiwi wild. Her nails dug into his muscular shoulders as he pressed his lower half to hers, pushing her hard against the ship. He broke the kiss momentarily and opened his mouth to talk.

"No," she said. "Just be with me, Ballou."

"I want to, but we have to talk." He stalled their kisses. "I don't want whatever is between us to be something you do in passing. I want to know there is a future to this."

Closing her eyes a second, she sighed. "I can't promise you that. Especially not after seeing—"

"Who? Seeing who, Kiwi? Is it another man?" Conell asked, his entire body tight.

Kiwi silently cursed herself for slipping up about Captain Ajos. "No one. You should go now. I have work to do."

"No." He thrust his body against hers, his cock striking her clit just right, making her breath catch. "Talk to me, Kiwi. Tell me the truth. Give me something about you. Something that tells me who you really are."

"I'm who you see before you." As she said it, she realized he wasn't buying it.

He stroked her cheek. "Please. My life is an open book to you. All I'm asking for is a peek between the pages of yours."

She put her forehead to his chin. "What do you want to know?"

"How about this man you just mentioned."

She would have answered but the alerts sounded, indicating an approaching vessel. Kiwi did what came naturally, she rushed to the arms cabinet on the maintenance bay, keyed in her code and opened it, pulling out what she thought she might need. Since the vessel they were on had turned into a safe haven on the outer quadrants for refugees of the war between humanoids and Vanos, they'd stopped meeting boarding guests in the receiving area and started routing them through the various landing bays. The hope was, if an enemy were to arrive by means of infiltrating a trusted ally, the ship and its occupants would have time to get ready to defend themselves.

As she strapped on extra ammunition, Conell shook his head. "How is it that something as tiny as you is so damn lethal?"

"I'm not sure." She smiled. "Just lucky I guess. Pick your poison."

"Ah, I'm a step ahead of you." He turned, allowing her a view of the P893 G-pulse gun he had tucked in the back of his pants.

"Nice." She was impressed. Conell, while brilliant with a body that screamed solider, had the heart of an academic. That only served to make her like him more, but Kiwi kept that to herself. He didn't need anything more in the way of encouragement. Besides, she'd already ridden him until he'd exploded in her, not once, but twice.

"If I start carrying a backup weapon too, will you tell me your real name?" he asked, helping her strap the ammunition belt over her shoulder.

"Why do you keep insisting Kiwi isn't my name?"

It wasn't, but she was curious to know how he'd figured it out.

A shrug was his only reply.

She made a move to pass him, but Conell caught her arm and held her in place. Her body tingled at his touch. Reaching out, he ran the pad of his thumb over the corner of her mouth, making her skin burn with delight. "Woman, I think I'm falling in love with you."

Kiwi tipped her head into his palm and closed her eyes, enjoying his touch more than she should. Her lips naturally puckered in hopes more was to come, and she had to pull herself out of her needy state and focus. "Hmm?"

"I said," he stroked her cheek, "you had some grease on you."

When Kiwi opened her eyes, she found Conell's face so close she could have kissed him. The sound of the adjacent hanger's doors opening was the only thing preventing her from carrying out the action.

"I didn't hear anyone grant permission for someone to dock."

Conell stared at her a moment before resignation clicked. "Neither did I."

He pushed past her, rushing in the direction of the adjacent hanger. She watched with a sick feeling in the pit of her stomach as Conell walked right out and in front of the hanger doors. She seized hold of his waistband and yanked him backwards, utilizing the strength of her reconditioned arm. Thanks to Aeron, it had been successfully repaired. There had been a fear of her body rejecting it but that hadn't been the case. A sensor had come loose. The operation to fix it was non-intrusive and Kiwi had been up and ready to go within hours.

Conell yelped and barely avoided falling. She hadn't meant to use that much strength.

"Kiwi?"

She put a finger to her lips to silence him and pointed at the doors. "Standing directly in front of them when I open them is a great way to get blown to pieces. If you'd prefer to go back and take your chances, then by all means, please do."

Pulling the gun from the back of his pants, he smiled down at her, looking nothing short of adorable. "No. I'm good. Thank you."

Kiwi sighed and motioned for him to lower his weapon. He did and she clicked his safety off. He wasn't going to shoot anything with it still on. "And people keep swearing to me you're brilliant."

"I am until I get around you, and then I'm lucky to form a complete sentence." He fluttered his eyelids and smiled. "You take my thoughts away."

"Do you ever stop?"

He nudged her. "Will you agree to run off to the nearest union moon and let me stake my claim on you legally?"

"Nope," she said, focusing on the doors, assuming Conell was being Conell and joking.

"Well, there is your answer then."

She punched in the sequence to open the doors and waited a second before turning slowly, going to one knee and aiming her weapon. The moment her sights locked on a Star Union transport vessel, she let off the trigger and waited to see if it was a trap or not. The Vanos were known for underhanded maneuvers. This would simply be another in a long line of them.

Conell tried to walk past her but she grabbed his hand and pulled him down next to her. "What? They're friendly."

"Only according to the stamp on the side of the ship. How do you know who's onboard?"

Conell stared at her with something akin to worry and admiration. "In your past life were you a military commander or a spy? Maybe a dictator of a small planet?"

"All of the above." She realized she still had hold of his hand and refused to let go. Instead, she laced her fingers through his and gave a

MAGNETIC ATTRACTION   69

gentle squeeze. "What about you? What were you in your past life?"

"Brilliant, of course."

She would have commented but the Star Union's hatch opened. The second Kiwi spotted a tall man with sandy-blond hair and a body that rivaled Conell's, her breath caught. She stood quickly, her finger near the trigger once more as she advanced on the man.

"Hands in the air!"

"Kiwi, no!" Conell yelled, trying to catch hold of her.

She slipped past his grasp and kept her weapon trained on the man before her. The man's turquoise gaze landed on her and his eyes widened.

"Put your *facq'elnin'* hands in the air. Now!"

"Kiwi, don't shoot. He's on our side," Conell said, putting himself between her and the man—leaving his brilliance in question once more.

She fought for air that didn't seem to want to come as she stared past Conell at the newcomer. It simply could not be the same man she'd once known. He was dead. That meant, this one was a Vanos imposture. She'd heard of them going to great lengths to try to assume another's identity thought she'd never realized how accurately they could pull it off. "Move, Conell."

The man stepped out from behind Conell with his hands in the air. As shock moved over his handsome face, Kiwi felt something deep within her breaking. Her time spent at the mercy of the enemy was still fresh in her mind. Seeing this ghost from the past wasn't helping.

"No," the man whispered. "It can't be." He went to lower his hands and she jerked her weapon, unsure now if she was actually willing to use it.

"Who are you?"

He lifted a brow. "Who are *you*?"

"Guys?" Conell looked back and forth between them. "This is ridiculous. Darrin, this is Kiwi. Kiwi, Darrin. Think we can put the weapons down and act like normal, non-violent people? I realize it would be a stretch for you both, but reach deep, folks. I think you can do it."

"Kiwi?" Darrin repeated a second before he seized hold of Conell's weapon and trained it on her.

Conell made a move to go at the man but Darrin shook his head. "No, Conell. Stay back. She's not safe to be near."

Kiwi stared harder at Darrin, unable to believe her eyes. "It can't be you. I watched you…" Tears fought to come but she held tight to them as she stared at a man she'd long thought dead.

Darrin shook his head. "Stop screwing with my mind. You're not her. You can't be. I went back and she was dead. They'd… After they'd… You're not her!"

The tears broke free. "What? You got away and then you came back? Are you stupid, Darrin?"

He tossed the weapon aside and stormed towards her. Kiwi didn't shoot. She couldn't even if she'd wanted to. Darrin pushed the barrel of her gun away from him and touched her redone arm lightly. "H-how?"

Kiwi dropped her weapon and tossed her arms around his neck. He was as tall as Conell, and the moment he stood, he lifted her off the ground and spun her around in a circle. "Oh gods, Kisenia, I thought you were dead. I searched everywhere for you. How are you here? How are you alive? How are you in one piece? How did you get away?"

Tears continued to fall as she clung to Darrin.

He stopped and held her firm to him. "Your family thinks you're dead. Your dad will—"

"No. No one can know, Darrin."

"Why?"

"That is the question of the hour," Conell said, his voice even. "That among others."

Kiwi wiped her cheeks and patted Darrin's shoulders. "Put me down."

"Hell no. I spent three years thinking you were dead, Kisenia. I'll be damned if I let go of you now." He chuckled. "All this time I thought you were gone and you've been shacked up here, with Conell? I should have known you'd find a posh life somewhere. You were always the belle of the ball."

She knew Darrin was only joking, but she couldn't stop herself from spilling things she never thought she'd reveal to anyone. "I haven't been free for three years, Darrin. I've been free for a year and a half. The first six months of which I spent running. They seemed to be able to find me anywhere I went." She let out a

MAGNETIC ATTRACTION   73

choked laugh, but was far from jovial. "Trust me, if you spend enough time at their mercy and then running for your life, you get stars smart real fast." She shoved off him and landed on her feet with ease. "You also push the thoughts from your head about the life you did have, the one you thought you were entitled to, and you stare reality in the face."

He paled. "The Vanos had you for over a year? That means when I went back for you… when the guards I captured told me you were dead…"

"They were lying. Think about it, Darrin, do you believe any of them would really let me die? Without me, they'd lose a valuable bargaining tool."

"Someone want to tell me what the hell is going on and why he keeps calling you Kisenia?" Conell stepped forward, glaring, and put his hand out to her.

Without thought, she took it and let out a deep breath. "Because it's my name. Kisenia Wise, or the nickname I had when I was little —Kiwi."

Suddenly, Kiwi felt guilty for keeping that detail from him over the last several months.

The hurt look in his eyes told her he too was upset with the fact it took a third party to bring about the revelation. "But you can't tell anyone else here. Promise me. I can't go back. I can't ever go back."

Conell's brow knitted. "I'd never let the Vanos have you back, Kiwi." He pulled her into his arms and held her close. "Never."

"Not them, Conell. I can't go home…" a rather dramatic breath fell from her lips, "…to my family."

"Your father never recovered from your, uhh, death, Kisenia." Darrin stepped towards her. "Your mother doesn't let anyone speak your name, and whenever she sees me, she cries."

Kiwi had spent many a day thinking of her family. Thinking of how they were. If they thought she was dead. She'd briefly considered going back to her home planet, simply to look in on them, but couldn't bring herself to do it. The shame in having been captured and for how many times she'd nearly broken, almost telling the Vanos what they wanted to know, kept her from going back. "I can't, Darrin. Please don't ask me to."

MAGNETIC ATTRACTION   75

"They won't look at you differently, Kisenia. You're their daughter, they'll—"

She jerked away from Conell and shook her head, an array of emotions washing over her. "Kiwi! Not Kisenia! Kisenia doesn't exist anymore, Darrin. She died in a Vanos prison camp and left me in her place. I'm not the same girl I was. I'm not the same naïve young woman who smiled when spoken to and who did whatever it was her father told her to do. I'm not the same person who agreed to let her parents arrange a marriage for her because it was expected of me, and I'm sure in stars' name not the woman you met in the watering station three and half years ago."

Darrin put his hands up. "Kisenia…erm… Kiwi, please. I understand you're not the same person, but that doesn't mean your parents shouldn't know you're alive."

"Why? So they can pick up where they left off, marrying me off to some professor who, from the way you were acting when you first arrived for me, wasn't even aware he was getting a bride?"

Darrin's gaze moved to Conell. "I think he's come around."

Hysterical laughter fell free from her lips. "Right, and now he'd want a woman who spent a year and a half of her life being tortured, just because of whose daughter she is and because of what she carries in her." She yanked at the ammunitions clip and pulled it away in a frenzy. "He'd want a woman who isn't a full humanoid? One who is not only part synthetic, but who found out, while being held prisoner, that she isn't even her parents' biological child?"

"What?"

She laughed harder, sounding anything but amused. "Oh yeah, I was just as shocked when their doctors came in, shoving the results of my DNA testing in my face. Daddy's little girl, his little princess, wasn't even really his, Darrin. Apparently, I'm the product of a Vanos and humanoid mating. I'm an unwanted bastard born from the same line of things that beat me until I couldn't move, who tried to kill the human in me. Who thought of that part as weak and were bound and determined to make me into something fit for their captain."

Darrin looked as if he was going to throw up. "You mean to tell me that sick son of a bitch, Ajos, wanted to keep you for himself?"

She stared at him. "Did you miss the part about me not being fully human?"

He waved a hand dismissively. "Yeah, I knew that about five minutes after I met you. At first I thought you had on some sort of perfume," he blushed, "that left me wanting to pin you to a wall. After a while, I realized I sensed something in you. Something familiar. Then I also realized something else." His gaze went to Conell. "You were entirely too perfect for the man you'd been selected for. You, with your nose always in a book, always eager to learn, were exactly what the doctor ordered. Pun intended."

She snorted. "Yeah, me, a real gal wonder, took to reading Vanos manuals whenever I could get my hands on one. Almost all were about combat, some sort of military thing or another. Some—" she touched her grease-covered backside, "—were on how to fix and fly ships. So, you tell me the truth, Darrin. Could the man my parents decided I'd spend the rest of my life with really want me?"

"I don't know."

She got a hold of her emotions. "At least you're honest."

Darrin locked gazes with Conell. "Why don't you ask him?"

"Right. I'll pick up a com and make an interstellar call to him right now. How should I identity myself? Should I tell him the ambassador's daughter is phoning? The woman his parents and my parents apparently thought was perfect for him? Or, how about the half-human, half-Vanos woman who is now sporting fake body parts because the men holding her prisoner thought they'd take a sledge hammer to her each and every time she refused to acknowledge their captain as her master?"

"Kiwi," Darrin cleared his throat, "you should know something about the man I was sent to take you to."

"What? Is he a Vanos fleet captain too?"

"He's part Vanos," Darrin said softly. "The same as me."

She stilled. "That's his worst thing? So, I have all this baggage and the worst he has is that he's part Vanos? Gods, a huge chunk of the crew here are. I thought I'd hate being around anyone who reminded me of them but..." she glanced at Conell, "...the idea of leaving these people terrifies me."

MAGNETIC ATTRACTION   79

Darrin laughed. "Uh, no. He has much more wrong with him. He's an ass. He's full of himself. He's way too smart for his own good. He's…"

"Pfft, he sounds like Conell." As she said it, she realized Conell was there, hearing everything she said. Her stomach cramped as shame washed over her. "I-I have to go. I need to clean up and—"

"What is said here stays here." Conell stepped closer and drew her into his embrace.

Kiwi almost yelled at him about not wanting his pity, but she realized his hold was exactly what she needed. She wasn't sure how much time passed with her clinging to him, but when she finally pulled away, she said nothing as she walked out of the hanger and headed for her cabin.

NINE

Conell watched as the woman he'd fallen in love with walked away. She was so tiny and petite in comparison to him that he often wanted to pull her into his arms and shelter her from the world. He couldn't explain his behavior before learning she'd been selected for him, nor had he tried, but after hearing the exchange between her and Darrin, he understood.

He locked gazes with a man he knew well. "Tell me everything."

"She should be the one to tell you."

"Darrin, don't. She won't and you know it." He let out a long, shaky breath, stunned his brother knew more about Kiwi than he did. "Start at the beginning. You know, the part where Mom and Dad arranged for me to be married but didn't feel the need to tell me."

His older brother sighed. "You spent so long denying the Vanos part of us that they were afraid you wouldn't look for your mate. That you'd ignore the urges and keep your nose buried in a book, so they took it upon themselves to find her."

His mate?

He'd heard of such a thing—that the Vanos, unlike humanoids, had a perfect someone they were compatible with. Sure, they could breed, even care for another, but in the end, legends told of how each had a lifemate, a perfect match roaming the universe. Being a man of science, Conell put little to no stock in legends. His parents knew him well. He'd have laughed at the idea of having a mate.

That was the old Conell. The new one had a nagging feeling there was truth behind the tales. From the very moment he'd laid eyes on the stubborn girl with a hot temper and a quick wit, his cock had been in a permanent state of erection. He hadn't been joking when he told Kiwi he was a smart man until he was around her and then he suddenly had trouble forming sentences.

Conell would spend countless hours watching her from afar, memorizing every curve of her heart-shaped face and every fleck of color sprinkled through her eyes. Brad, a long-time friend and the commander of the vessel, often teased him about laws being in place to prevent men from following women around, but Conell couldn't help himself.

"How did Mom and Dad find her?"

Darrin shut the hatch to his Star Union vessel. "They didn't. Her father found them. He said his daughter was plagued by recurring dreams and that she talked in her sleep. He also mentioned she had no memory of them upon waking. They brought in a sleep expert and they hooked her up to a viewing machine."

Conell had heard of the technique. It allowed people to see what the person dreaming was seeing. "And?"

Darrin grinned. "And apparently, she was dreaming of your sorry self. You know—" Darrin winked, "home, hubby, two kids. The works. I guess when they spotted your university nametag, they hunted you down. Our parents decided the best way to ensure you'd meet with her would be to simply drop her off on your doorstep with the news she was to be your wife."

Conell tried to soak in all the information. "And you were who they selected to be her escort?"

"No, when I heard about what was going on, I volunteered to stop—it was halfway between her and you—and pick her up. None of us knew the Vanos had invaded the station. We walked into a trap. We were all held prisoner for a period of time." He pointed in the direction Kiwi had left. "Some more than others."

He was quiet for a moment. "Darrin, you've had three years to tell me about her. Why didn't you?"

His brother looked at him as if he were mad. "What the hell good would come of me telling you I not only met your future wife, your lifemate, but that I wasn't able to save her?"

"Kiwi doesn't know we're brothers. Can we keep it that way for a while?" Conell stared off in the distance, his mind racing with this new knowledge about Kiwi.

"We can, but will Aeron and Brad?"

Conell thought about how much his friends

wanted him happy and how much Aeron had pushed him to make a move with Kiwi. He smiled. "They will. Now, tell me more about Kisenia Wise. I want to know everything, Darrin."

"I think that part should come from her. Not me."

He didn't argue with his brother. Instead, he pulled a crate up and took a seat, preparing himself for a long overdue talk.

TEN

Kiwi stood, uneasy, staring around the planetside restaurant. When Aeron had all but insisted they head there to celebrate Darrin's arrival, Kiwi wanted to hide away in her cabin. Aeron, the proud new mother of a beautiful two-month-old son, had a horrible case of cabin fever. Unable to deny her friend, Kiwi had agreed. When Aeron pulled out an evening gown with the intention of forcing Kiwi into it, Kiwi tried to renege. Unfortunately, it didn't work.

She glanced towards her blonde friend, who was currently on the arm of her husband. Aeron gave her a wide smile. "You look amazing, Kiwi."

Brad kissed the top of his wife's head. "I

have to hand it to you, Aeron, I wasn't entirely sure Kiwi was a girl under all that grease."

"Ha, ha," Kiwi mused. "Don't make me punch you in the gut again, pretty boy."

"Pretty boy?" Brad's jaw dropped. "I have never been—"

Aeron patted his arm and laughed. "Honey, it's almost too easy for her to push your buttons."

"Shouldn't she be off in a corner, fidgeting and demanding to get back into her stained work pants?" Brad grinned over the top of his wife's head.

Kiwi stuck her tongue out at him. It was childish, but when he returned the movement, she realized he was a big kid too.

Brad laughed. "You know, you remind me of me at times, Kiwi."

"Great," Aeron huffed. "I don't think I can handle two of you."

A strong, warm arm slid around Kiwi's waist. "Oh, the two of you are so very mature."

Kiwi sucked in a deep breath. Aeron had told her Conell couldn't make it down, that he had a meeting planned with several of the other scientists. As she looked to her side to find him standing there, dressed for the occasion, she couldn't think. Couldn't speak. She'd always known he was the type who would flourish in a setting such as this one, but in no way could she have been prepared for just how handsome he truly was.

Conell bent down and pressed his mouth to her ear. "Show him your combat boots, *delicatica*. That'll teach him."

A tiny giggle erupted from her. "I can't." She lifted the gown, revealing a pair of clear heels. "Aeron confiscated them and left these in their place."

Conell's laughter bubbled around her. She'd thought he might behave strangely around her, having heard the truth of her past, but he seemed to be himself. He pulled her closer to him. "Mmm, let's have Brad and Aeron get the table. Come on."

He didn't allow her to protest as he led her out and onto the dance floor. He was dancing gracefully with her before she could so much as blink and, truth be told, it felt wonderful. Kiwi missed little things like this. Things that made her feel feminine, sexy and desired, but most of all, safe.

Conell led masterfully, as if he were a seasoned pro. He twirled her in a circle before yanking her against his body. The feel of him pressed so close to her left her panting and positive the temperature in the room had skyrocketed. She put her cheek to his chest and closed her eyes, imagining what it would have been like to meet Conell before her attack. He was exactly the type of man she'd have fallen for. Hell, she *had* fallen for him.

He increased their pace, taking the dance, based loosely on original Earth waltzing mixed with an old dance from the Eros region, to a new level. Kiwi held firm to him and matched him step for step, laughing as Conell twirled her in a circle.

When the music stopped, she went to her tiptoes, tugged on him for him to bend down, and planted a kiss on his cheek. "Thank you, Conell."

"No." He kissed the tip of her nose. "Thank you, Kiwi."

She blushed, the look in his eyes reminded her of the night she'd surrendered her body to him.

He touched her cheek and bent, putting his

MAGNETIC ATTRACTION 91

mouth to her ear. "I want to be in you again. You have no idea how badly."

"Oh…" she fanned her face, "…I think I know."

He grinned, eyeing up a back hall. He lifted a brow in question.

Kiwi bit her lower lip. "Conell, they'll be waiting for us to join them at the table."

He kissed her cheek. "I like hearing my name on your lips, Kisenia."

She wanted to chastise him for saying her real name in public, but instead she went to her tiptoes and pressed her lips to his. He didn't seem to care that they were in the middle of an upscale restaurant. He devoured her mouth and she let him.

He drew back a bit. "If you didn't have the history you do, would you leave with Darrin to meet the man your parents wanted you to marry?"

She paused, surprised he'd taken the conversation there. "But I do have the history I do." She ran a finger over his lower lip. "And it's not fair to ask me that when I'm standing here with you."

"Why?" he asked, the look on his face saying he already knew the answer.

"No reason."

He pulled her closer. "Answer me. I need to hear how you feel about me."

She gave him a look of longing. "Isn't it a little early to make any sort of declaration of feelings?"

She already knew how she felt about him, she just didn't want to risk her heart by telling him the truth. What if he rejected her? Worse yet, what if he didn't? He'd demand to know the intimate details of her time as a Vanos prisoner. She could never tell him about it. He wouldn't be able to look her in the eyes ever again. She already knew she had to confide in someone about Ajos and the threat he represented. That person couldn't be Conell. Telling him would mean he'd find out the ugly truth.

She tugged on his hand and knew from the look on his face that he was hurt by her inability to tell him what he meant to her. She bit her lower lip and then met his gaze. "I can't answer your question about leaving to meet the man my parents selected, because no matter how hard I try, I can't imagine having not met you, Conell. Do you understand what I'm saying?"

The slight up-curve of his lips told her he did.

He bent, kissing her gently. "That's all I needed to know, Kisenia."

ELEVEN

Ajos watched as his woman danced with the other man—one Dr. Conell Ballou. He'd had his men digging for information about the man since he'd last seen him with Kisenia. He'd learned the man was on a watch list of his government and considered a viable threat to the Vanos as a whole. He also learned that, for a brief time, he'd held the doctor's brother in his grasp. If all went as planned, he'd have not only the good doctor, but his brother again. The mass escapes were an embarrassment. A mar on his record. To retrieve them all again and to bring in an enemy of his people would leave his higher-ups in awe of his talents as a commanding officer.

Deep in thought, Ajos reflected upon the time when he'd had Kisenia all to himself to do with what he may—the days of breaking her spirit down, of watching her beg for her life and for that of the others held with her, of feeling her squirm beneath him, her soft body conforming to him, accepting him even though the fire of hate burned in her eyes. He longed for the return of the fight. The sheer pleasure of inflicting pain she shouldn't have been able to bear, only to find she could accept it and so very much more. Never had a female he'd taken prisoner given him so much fulfillment, so much joy. She was the ultimate game to play with. One he never tired of and who needed to be taught the lesson of a lifetime.

Soon. She'll be mine again and she will answer for leaving me…for betraying me with him.

His cock hardened at the sight of Kisenia there, picking at her food, the fork sliding over her lips. Lips he knew well. Lips he would soon know again.

She glanced in his direction for the briefest of moments but looked away, not seeing him.

Ajos tapped his communicator lightly,

gaining the attention of his men. "On my signal, move in and secure the female. I want the male she's with taken alive. He will pay for daring to touch what's mine, and in the end he'll know who she truly belongs to."

TWELVE

She sat, poking at the dish before her, knowing she should at least make an attempt at eating and appearing civil. Conell had gone out of his way to make this evening special. She couldn't shake the cloud of dread hanging over her. This was all too good, too perfect. Nothing in her life in the last three years was this way. Something tragic always followed. Seeing Ajos only one quadrant over still ate at her gut. One quadrant was hardly enough space between him and her. He was a madman and, if he held true to form, he'd be hunting her right now.

She glanced around, hating the way the windows in the restaurant reflected everything back at her. He could be there, lurking, watching, waiting for the right moment to strike. He'd go for Conell if Ajos knew what Conell meant to her.

She looked towards Aeron and Brad and noticed the way they watched one another. Brad hung on her every word, her every movement. Their newborn son was beautiful and healthy and their love for one another grew each day. A piece of Kiwi wished she had what they did—some sort of normalcy in the chaos.

The waiter came around, carrying a tray of drinks special to the restaurant. The man scanned each person prior to handing them a drink. Kiwi had seen the act done before in regard to drinks not native to humanoids. By using a handheld scanning device, the establishment could determine who could and who could not tolerate the beverage. The advent of such technology and processes certainly cut down on the number of eating-related deaths.

The waiter approached their table and scanned Brad. Nodding, he offered a drink to Brad before moving to Aeron. He paused and she blushed. "Yes, I'm lactating. And no, I don't want a drink. Thank you though."

MAGNETIC ATTRACTION   101

Brad and Conell chuckled. Kiwi looked sympathetically at her friend.

Aeron winked. "Have one for me, Kiwi."

The waiter gave Conell his and then scanned Kiwi. He stopped and bent his head, saying something in a language she didn't recognize. Since Brad and Conell were both fitted with translators, they understood him. Whatever he said made Brad's eyes widen and Conell turn and grab her to him.

Aeron nudged her husband. "What? I'm not fluent in his language. What did he say and why does Conell look like he might pass out or drag her out of here? Hmm, maybe both."

Kiwi looked to the waiter and then to Conell. "Ballou?"

He grabbed the drink that should have been hers and drank it in one giant gulp. Brad smacked his hand on the table and let out a rather long line of curses, spanning every language Kiwi knew plus some. "Aeron tried to tell me there was something there between the two of you. I told her she was reading too much into it." His voice hardened. "I was wrong."

Lost, Kiwi glanced at Aeron who appeared as clueless as she was.

Brad narrowed his gaze on Conell. "It better be you that's the—"

"It is," Conell answered flatly.

"And you better not have hurt her in any way. If you so much as—"

Conell pivoted in his seat. "Hurt her? Don't be a *takjon*, Fairbanks! There is no way in hell I'd ever hurt her."

"You're twice her size and I've seen the way she turns down your advances."

Kiwi pieced together at least a portion of what they were talking about and pushed back in her seat. "Whoa. Hold on a minute here. We —" she pointed from herself to Brad, "—are not discussing my personal life or Conell's."

"Oh, he's Conell to you now?" Brad set his drink down and ignored Aeron as she tried to calm him. "How many times have I walked past you, hearing you mumble about him being a cocky jerk?"

Conell stood slowly, looking lethal. "Tell me, Fairbanks, what the hell business is this of yours? You have a wife. Stop obsessing over mine."

Kiwi bumped the table so hard with her

MAGNETIC ATTRACTION   103

rebuilt arm that she made her plate flip over. She stared up at Conell. "W-wife? I'm not your—"

He pointed at her. "Quiet. This is between Fairbanks and me."

Her jaw dropped. She stood, pushing past him, making sure to give an extra shove as she went. He tripped but didn't fall.

Pity.

Seething mad and thoroughly confused, Kiwi stormed towards the restrooms. She rounded the corner, making her way down the long corridor. Conell was suddenly there, spinning her around and pinning her to the wall. Kiwi opened her mouth to yell but he pressed his hand over her lips.

"I'm sorry. I didn't mean to order you around and act that way. I'm just...I'm absorbing, that's all."

"Absorbing what?" she asked, not following.

His gaze slid down the length of her and a slow smile moved over his face. "Kisenia, would you... Could you at least think about... What I mean to say is...oh, hell."

He kissed her so thoroughly her toes curled.

She found herself being lifted off the floor and carried down the hall. Conell kicked the button to open a side door and then carried her through it. Kiwi stopped kissing him back long enough to notice they were in a storage room of sorts.

"Ballou?"

Grinning mischievously, he pressed her to the wall and returned to caressing her tongue with his. He wasn't gentle about it and she didn't want him to be. He lifted her gown, pulling on it as she continued swirling her tongue around his. Kiwi ran her hands through his hair, tugging on it, wanting him even closer.

Moisture pooled between her legs and she smiled against his mouth, remembering what it was like to have his cock inside her, moving in and out of her. She wanted everything he'd willingly give her.

The higher he lifted her gown, the damper she became. His fingers found her slit and she moaned as he eased her panties aside and entered her. He felt around, deep within her, making her body spring with need. She searched his mouth with her tongue. He pulled his drenched fingers from her core and brought them to his lips. The look of ecstasy in his green eyes encouraged her, making her bold.

Kiwi purred and rubbed against him. "More."

The door to the storage room opened and Conell yanked her gown down, covering any signs of what they'd been doing.

Brad appeared, followed closely by Aeron, who looked helpless. She stared at Conell. "Can we please go back to the ship?"

Brad glared at Conell before turning that same look upon Kiwi. "Get up to that ship, young lady. And don't even think of coming out of your quarters."

Aeron smacked his arm. "Brad! You're acting like you're her father. What's going on? I know damn well you're nowhere near old enough to be and I, for one, know exactly where you've been since you were a teenager."

Brad exhaled slowly just as Conell moved Kiwi behind him in a protective manner.

"I don't know what's wrong with me. When I heard that waiter's reason for refusing her the drink, all I could think about was locking her away from men and killing the guy who did that to her." He stared at Conell. "Ballou, we've had our differences, but we've known each other a long damn time. You're a good guy. I know that. It's just…something's making me a little over-protective of her. I can't explain it."

Kiwi grabbed Conell's hand with her recon-ditioned one and squeezed. He yelped and tried to pry her fingers free of his. "K-Kiwi."

"What's wrong? Why didn't I get the drink?" She yanked on Conell's hand.

The sounds of someone shouting came from the outer corridor. Brad and Conell ran out to see what it was, leaving Kiwi and Aeron in the storage room. Aeron offered a loving smile. "Conell is a fabulous guy."

"I know. Any reason why you're picking now to point that out?"

Aeron frowned. "You mean you really don't know?"

"Uh, know what?"

Brad rushed back into the storage room. "Aeron, you and Kiwi get to the ship and take it back to the main vessel. Darrin's here with a team. A unit of Vanos guards are here. They're headed this way. We'll handle the Vanos."

MAGNETIC ATTRACTION   107

Kiwi knew then who was leading the Vanos guards.

Ajos.

She also knew he wanted her and no one else. Risking her friends' lives wasn't something she could do. She nodded and then motioned Brad closer. He came and she drew back her fist, hitting him hard in the face. He went down fast. Aeron screamed and Kiwi ran from the room. Closing the door, she took a deep breath before punching a hole in the opening unit, effectively jamming the door.

Conell came around the corner. "Where is Fairbanks? He said he was getting you and Aeron to safety and—"

She pointed in the opposite direction. "He went that way. Aeron was right behind him. I wanted to find you."

For a second, she thought his head might pop clean off. "You what?"

He grabbed her hand in his and ran in the direction of the back exit. They burst into the food-preparation area and she yanked hard on him, slinging his body towards the open food-station room. The moment he stumbled in, Kiwi used her rebuilt arm to slam the door shut tight. Conell would be able to get out but the tiny distraction would allow her enough time to find Ajos first—hopefully sparing the life of the man she loved.

Loved?

Kiwi pushed thoughts of her feelings for him from her head and ran, kicking off her heels along the way. Out of nowhere, she was snatched up by Darrin. He held tight to her. "Kisenia, I know what you're doing and it won't work. Ajos won't just take you and leave them. He'll slaughter them to prove a point. Especially Conell."

She froze. "He's evil."

He set her down slowly, keeping a close eye on her. "I know. So does Conell, but he doesn't know what the guy looks like. I do. When I spotted him on a digital-memory capture from another crewmember at the watering hole, I knew he'd be a problem for us. I also knew the minute you found out a Vanos unit was coming for you, you'd sacrifice yourself to save everyone else.

"Conell knows about Ajos?" she asked, sickened.

"I do, baby."

She spun and found Conell there. Brad rushed in behind him, looking winded and pissed. He pointed at Kiwi. "I will take you over my knee if you ever pull a stunt like that again."

Kiwi couldn't help but grin at the sight of his bruised cheek. "Might want to put some ice on that."

"Or," a deep voice that sent chills through her said, "I would suggest you all come with me like good little pieces of trash."

Kiwi tensed. Conell made a move to come at her and the sound of a pulse gun being cocked alerted her that he would be shot.

"No!" She twisted to stare at Ajos. She didn't wait, choosing instead to run straight for Conell, putting her body in front of his. "Don't hurt him!"

Conell picked her up and thrust her behind him with a growl.

Ajos laughed. "She is a stubborn one, isn't she? Do you know what else she is?" He smiled. "She's a nice, tight little cunt who screams when you—"

Conell went to lunge at Ajos, and he fired. At that exact moment, Brad charged Ajos from the side, knocking into him, making the shot go wild. It pierced a vat of something, causing it to ooze at a slow pace. Since they were standing in a storage room of a restaurant, no one panicked at what might have been released.

Kiwi reached under Conell's suit jacket and grabbed his pulse gun. She had it out and aimed at Ajos in record time. Conell made a move to take it from her but Darrin intervened. "No, little brother, let her do this."

Little brother?

She stared between the men, suddenly realizing how very much they looked alike.

Ajos laughed, appearing unafraid of them all. "My men will be here shortly. You will all rot in a prison, knowing your women belong to me."

"Actually," Darrin said, "your men have most likely met up with our men and the only thing that will be rotting is your corpse. But that's only my take on it. Feel free to ignore me."

Kiwi's hand began to shake. It wasn't even the rebuilt one. Staring down the barrel of a gun, looking into the eyes of a monster, horrific memories surfaced.

MAGNETIC ATTRACTION   111

"Kisenia," Conell whispered. "Let me do this."

"No." Her hand continued to shake. "I can do it. I have to do it."

He put his hand over hers. "It's my place to protect you. I should have been there with you from the start. It shouldn't have been Darrin coming to escort you. It should have been me."

All she could do was stare at him. "Why you?"

"Because…"

Darrin nodded. "Because he's the man I was taking you to meet, Kisenia. He's the man your parents selected for you."

Speechless, she felt denial creeping through her and her hand shook even more. Conell eased the weapon from her hand and tossed it to Darrin. "Shooting him is too kind. I think I'll use my bare hands."

"I'll help," Darrin said.

Brad stepped forward. "Me too."

Kiwi almost walked away, letting them handle it completely. But the memory of her time with that monster centered her fears and emotions. She moved forward fast, dodging Conell's grasp a second before she drew her reconditioned arm back and punched as hard as she could. Her fist connected with Ajos's groin, and she didn't need the screams he let out as verification she had her revenge.

Doesn't mean I don't enjoy hearing them, though.

Strong arms pulled her away from Ajos. She knew it was Conell and she welcomed the intervention. While she could and did assure Ajos could never again do what he'd done to her, she didn't have it in her to kill him. Something told her that Conell, however, did have what it would take, and for that she was grateful.

Conell kissed Kiwi's temple and raked his gaze down her. "This time, really take Aeron back to the ship. I don't want either of you hurt, and I especially don't want our baby injured."

"Our what?"

Conell grinned. "Our little one. You're pregnant. It's why the waiter wouldn't serve you that drink."

"Ohmygods. I'm…? We're…? A baby?"

"Think that's shocking, wait until you hear about how our contract of marriage, which I wasn't aware my presence wasn't needed for, was not only submitted to the magistrate system three years prior by our parents, it was witnessed." He bent down and pressed his mouth to hers. "That just means you are my wife, and apparently we've been married for three years."

The room seemed to spin before her legs gave out on her and darkness swept in.

THIRTEEN

Conell crawled onto the bed, over his wife, and kissed her cheeks until her eyes opened. She yawned and then smiled. He never tired of waking her up with kisses and he never tired of seeing her belly swollen with their child. "It's time to get up. They'll be here within the hour."

Kiwi looked nervous. "I can't do it. Tell them we changed our minds."

"I am not telling my mother that we're not saying our vows in front of them. She's damn scary when pushed too far. From what Darrin tells me, your father isn't exactly a guy I should piss off either."

"But Conell…"

He touched the tiny swell of her stomach. "Kiwi, they've given us time together. Almost three full months. They need this. They need to see you and hug you, know that you really are alive and well. They may not be your biological parents, but they love you like they are. And they want to know their decision three years back—to send you to me—wasn't the wrong one. They were right. We do belong together and nothing stopped that from happening."

He skimmed his hand up her body, loving the fact she slept naked every night. He cupped a breast and then bent, licking her nipple. She arched into him and opened her legs automatically. Conell knew she'd be wet and ready for him. She always was. He lined up with her entrance and thrust in, careful to keep his weight supported with his arms and off her stomach.

"You feel so good, *delicatica*."

She smiled lazily at him before lifting her head and kissing him. Her cunt grasped his cock, drawing animalistic noises from him as he pummeled into her. Conell fucked her mouth with his tongue, thrusting his tongue in and out to match the movements of his hips. With a

MAGNETIC ATTRACTION   117

groan, he reached down, lifting one of her legs higher, going even deeper into her.

Kiwi cried out his name as her nails bit into his back.

Conell smiled against her mouth, excited at how passionate a lover she was. She clawed at him.

"Harder."

He obliged, ramming into her warmth. He moved his hand just enough that the tips of his fingers reached the cleft of her ass. Her eyes widened a second before he dipped a finger into her anus. A fire lit in him as he remembered the night before, when he'd taken her there after fucking her sweet mouth.

Kiwi bucked, her pussy shuddering around his shaft.

He kept going. Kept thrusting into her. Kept pushing his finger deeper into her ass. The minute his orgasm struck and seed shot forth into her, filling her, tremors wracked his body. Conell tossed his head back and let out a battle cry as he continued to empty his seed into her. She came once more, screaming his name and digging her nails even deeper into his back.

The door to their bedroom opened fast.

"I'm positive something is wrong! I heard screaming and… Oh dear, I, umm… Conell? Darling?"

He froze. "Mom?"

Kiwi's brown eyes twinkled as she burst into laughter.

Sheepishly, Conell glanced over his shoulder to find his mother staring at him. Darrin was next to her, his face beat red and his lips trembling with pending laughter.

"Mom, I'll be out in a minute," he snapped.

She waved her hand dismissively. "Oh, nonsense. I gave birth to you. You don't have anything I haven't seen before. I would like to meet my daughter-in-law, so hurry up and finish."

"Mom."

Darrin came to his rescue. "Uh, Mom, let's give them some privacy. They'll meet us in the main receiving room."

"Fine. We should probably go find Kisenia's parents. You don't think they're still going on and on with Brad about how they adopted Kisenia from his parents when she was just a baby, do you? Poor Brad. Such a good boy from such a horrible family. They never treated him or his siblings right, and to sell their youngest off…"

"Mom," Darrin said. "It's not our business. I'm sure they had their reasons and it worked out for the best."

Conell stared down at his wife. Gone was the look of mischief. What replaced it was a look of absolute shock. "That big demanding oaf is my brother?"

Laughing, Conell covered her face with kisses, listening as the sound of their outer quarter's doors closing filled the room. "Mmm, guess that explains his overprotectiveness and the fact the two of you tease each other like two little kids."

Kiwi wrapped her leg around his waist. "Conell, how fast can you be? I need you again before I can go out there and face them all."

"Anything for you, *delicatica*." He moved in and out of her slowly. "Have I told you today how much I love you?"

"No." She grinned. "But you're welcome to show me. And Conell?"

"Yes?"

"I love you too."

THE END

DEAR READER

Did you enjoy this title and want to know more about Mandy M. Roth, her pen names and all the titles she has available for purchase (over 100)?

About Mandy:

New York Times & *USA TODAY* Bestselling Author Mandy M. Roth is a self-proclaimed Goonie, loves 80s music and movies and wishes leg warmers would come back into fashion. She also thinks the movie The Breakfast Club should be mandatory viewing for...okay, everyone. When she's not dancing around her office to the sounds of the 80s or writing books, she can be found designing book covers for New York publishers, small presses, and indie authors. She also writes as Reagan Hawk, Kennedy Kovit and Rory Michaels.

Learn More:

To learn more about Mandy and her pen names, please visit http://www.mandyroth.com

For latest news about Mandy's newest releases and sales subscribe to her newsletter

To join Mandy's Facebook Reader Group: The Roth Heads, please visit

https://www.facebook.com/groups/Mandy-RothReaders/

Review this title:

Please let others know if you enjoyed this title. Consider leaving an honest review on the vendor site in which you purchased this title. Reviews help to spread the word and boost overall sales. This means more books in the series you love.

Thank you!

Lightning Source UK Ltd.
Milton Keynes UK
UKHW01f1836080818
326963UK00001B/128/P